USBORNE FANTASY PUZZLE BOOKS

STAR QUEST

Andy Dixon

Illustrated by
Nick Harris

Edited by
Felicity Brooks

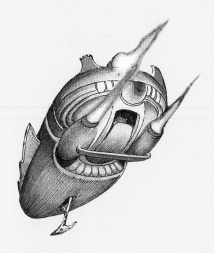

Cover and additional design by
Amanda Gulliver and Stephanie Jones

Earthspeak translation:

Greetings Earthlings!

Do not be alarmed. I come in peace.

My name is Plib. I have come from the small planet of Bliss in a galaxy far away. On behalf of the inhabitants of Bliss, I have come to deliver an important message and ask for your help.

Our planet, like your Earth, was once a nice place to live, but it is quickly becoming a frozen wasteland. Evil Lord Glaxx, leader of a group of intergalactic space thugs, named the Lava Louts, has developed a laser beam that can suck all the energy from stars. At this very moment he is draining the star which gives our planet all its heat and light. Without energy we shall all freeze and die in ice and darkness.

Glaxx's plan is to suck all the energy from stars throughout the universe and to destroy life on all planets. He must be stopped! It is only a matter of time before he reaches Earth and sucks the life from your star, the Sun.

If there is anyone on Earth brave and clever enough to help me and my planet, please join me on the greatest adventure of your life...

THE STAR QUEST.

With thanks, Plib

Important information for all questers

Thank you for volunteering to go on the Star Quest, and welcome to Star World – the most exciting leisure park on Planet Earth. Before you set off on the quest there are some things you need to know. Please study this information carefully and look at the picture of Planet Bliss at the bottom of this page.

What's the problem?

Evil Lord Glaxx, leader of the Lava Louts whose bodies are made entirely of molten lava, has developed a powerful laser that extracts the energy from stars. At this very moment he is in the process of draining the energy from a star that provides all the heat and light for a small planet called Bliss.

Why should I care?

It's only a matter of time before Lord Glaxx comes to our galaxy and turns his laser on our own star – the Sun. When he does, the Earth and everything on it will be frozen – forever!

Can Glaxx be stopped?

Only if you can find Plib, the messenger from Bliss, agree to help him track down Lord Glaxx, and put a stop to his evil exploits, can you help save the planet.

Can't someone else help?

There's room for two more Earthlings, as well as you, on board Plib's spaceship. The first two people that walk into the ship will accompany you, if Plib can persuade them to help him.

How soon do we have to go?

Now. Lord Glaxx will soon finish draining the star, leaving Planet Bliss just a freezing, lifeless ball in the depths of space. There's no time to lose.

How do we get there?

You'll set out from Star World in Plib's spacecraft and head for Planet Bliss far, far away.

THE PLANET OF BLISS

Jelly Stones

Blange

Ooh Aah Forest

Bliss's Star

Craterland

Tentacle Towers

Squirm Island

Loch Lung

Mug Swamp

Crystal Desert

Lava Mountains

Ice Lands

Glaxx's Ship

How to do the puzzles

The quest will be difficult and dangerous, so you will need skill, courage and the eyes of an eagle if you are to survive. In each place you visit you will see a panel similar to the one below. It explains what you have to do in that place before you can move on to the next stage of the quest.

Ice Lands

You escaped from the space station, but your ship was hit by the station's laser cannons and you were forced to make an emergency landing in Ice Lands on... Before Glaxx started draining energy from the star, most of the planet's crops were grown here. Now it's a frozen wasteland.

SAMPLE

Many of Glaxx's soldiers are here playing winter sports. You must find some clothes to keep warm and disguise yourselves. Find 4 pairs of snow boots, 4 pairs of goggles, 4 snow hats and 4 gooth skin coats. Don't take anything that the soldiers are wearing.

Plib's ship is damaged beyond repair and his home is on the other side of the mountains. Plib says there is a tunnel that will take you there. Find the entrance to the tunnel.

The snow is too deep to walk through, but you must reach the tunnel. There is an abandoned snow craft half buried in the snow. Find the snow craft and its handlebars, and also find a shovel to dig them out. Put them together and head for the tunnel.

Find a pot of melted gooth's cheese and 6 crusts of bread to take with you.

This tells you where you are.

These pictures and maps show you where each place is. Plib, the alien, has copies of all of them.

When it is time, read these pieces of information carefully. They contain some very important clues.

The pictures on the panels show creatures or things you have to find or avoid in each place you visit. Some will be very hard to spot, because you can only see a small part of them.

Some pictures show things you will need later in the quest, or ways of getting to the next place.

Somewhere on the panels are pictures of food and drinks to look for. You can find something to eat in nearly every place you visit.

Along the bottom of each page are some more pictures in squares. The numbers tell you how many of that thing you can spot in the main scene. Finding these things will sharpen your skills and help you survive the quest.

9 two-headed ponguins

how boards

Lord Glaxx

The energy crystals

After you have left Star World, you will need to find one energy crystal in each of the first seven places you visit. In the eighth place there are three crystals. You will need all ten crystals later to help you defeat Glaxx, so don't forget to look for them.

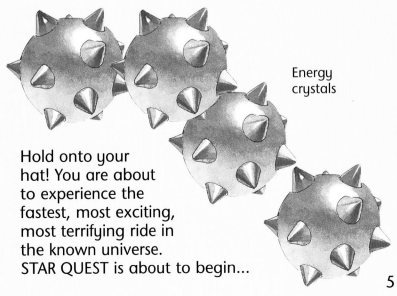

Energy crystals

Hold onto your hat! You are about to experience the fastest, most exciting, most terrifying ride in the known universe. STAR QUEST is about to begin...

Star World

You are at Star World, the biggest space theme park on Earth. You don't have time to go on any of the rides, because you must find Plib, who is the only real alien here. You also need to spot the two people who will be going with you on the Star Quest.

Plib is having trouble convincing anyone that his story is true. Soon he'll have to return to his spaceship. Can you spot him?

Two children, named Jess and Harry, are walking over to Plib's spaceship, thinking it's just another ride. Can you find them?

Jess wears red ribbons in her hair and carries a small, furry backpack in the shape of a dog.

Harry is very tall for his age and has red hair that he can never comb flat.

You won't be able to go anywhere unless you can find Plib's spaceship. Can you see it?

Can you find 5 starburgers and 5 solarshakes to take with you on the long journey?

7 space helmets

9 roadrunners

12 lollipops

14 Star World hats

10 security guards

9 prairie dogs

35 balloons

Plib's Ship

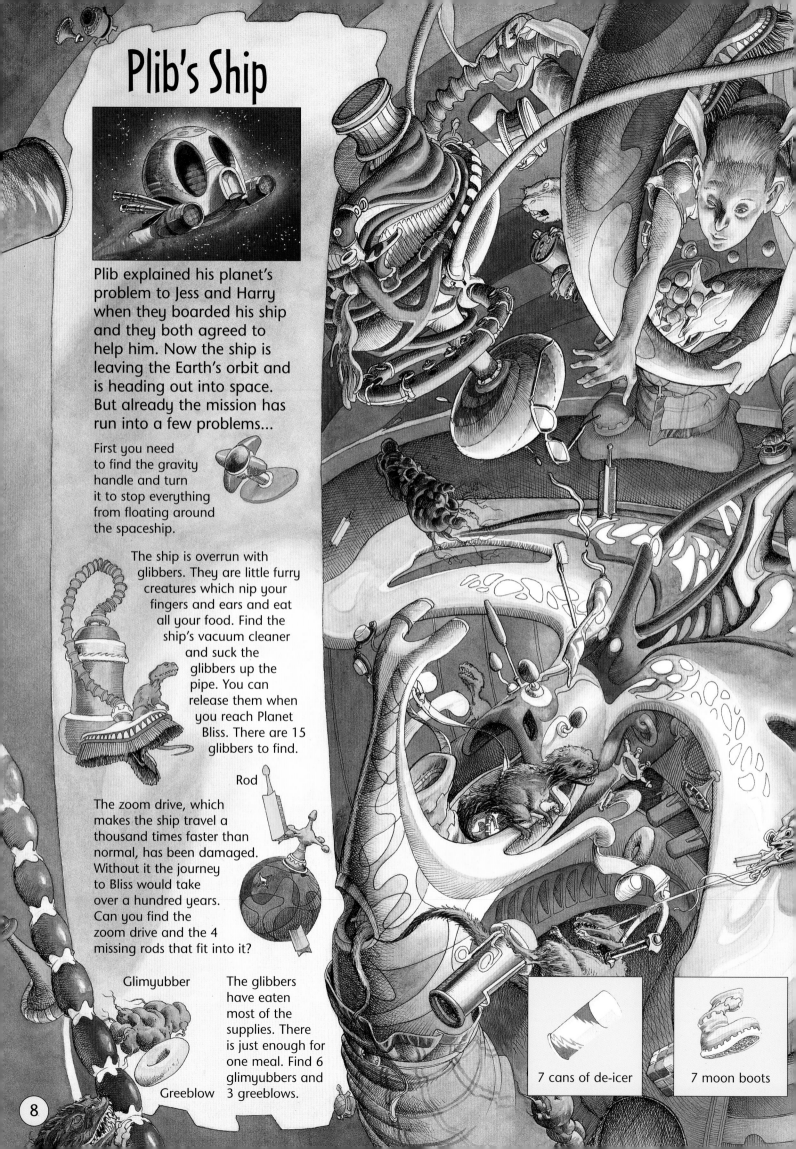

Plib explained his planet's problem to Jess and Harry when they boarded his ship and they both agreed to help him. Now the ship is leaving the Earth's orbit and is heading out into space. But already the mission has run into a few problems...

First you need to find the gravity handle and turn it to stop everything from floating around the spaceship.

The ship is overrun with glibbers. They are little furry creatures which nip your fingers and ears and eat all your food. Find the ship's vacuum cleaner and suck the glibbers up the pipe. You can release them when you reach Planet Bliss. There are 15 glibbers to find.

Rod

The zoom drive, which makes the ship travel a thousand times faster than normal, has been damaged. Without it the journey to Bliss would take over a hundred years. Can you find the zoom drive and the 4 missing rods that fit into it?

Glimyubber

Greeblow

The glibbers have eaten most of the supplies. There is just enough for one meal. Find 6 glimyubbers and 3 greeblows.

7 cans of de-icer

7 moon boots

5 pairs of goggles

14 spare fuses

4 travel blankets

6 music cylinders

17 air fresheners

Space Station

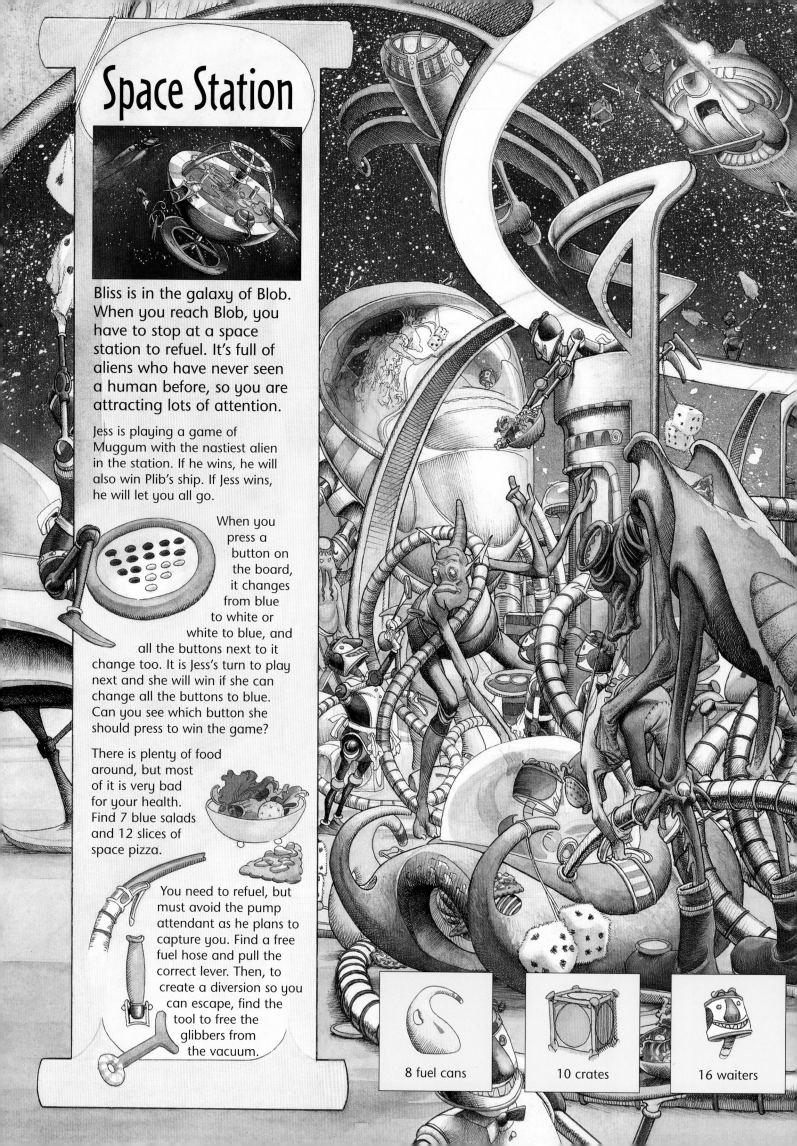

Bliss is in the galaxy of Blob. When you reach Blob, you have to stop at a space station to refuel. It's full of aliens who have never seen a human before, so you are attracting lots of attention.

Jess is playing a game of Muggum with the nastiest alien in the station. If he wins, he will also win Plib's ship. If Jess wins, he will let you all go.

When you press a button on the board, it changes from blue to white or white to blue, and all the buttons next to it change too. It is Jess's turn to play next and she will win if she can change all the buttons to blue. Can you see which button she should press to win the game?

There is plenty of food around, but most of it is very bad for your health. Find 7 blue salads and 12 slices of space pizza.

You need to refuel, but must avoid the pump attendant as he plans to capture you. Find a free fuel hose and pull the correct lever. Then, to create a diversion so you can escape, find the tool to free the glibbers from the vacuum.

8 fuel cans

10 crates

16 waiters

13 fuel tokens

4 keys

6 space horns

9 pairs of furry dice

7 glibber traps

11

Ice Lands

You escaped from the space station, but your ship was hit by the station's laser cannons and you were forced to make an emergency landing in Ice Lands on Bliss. Before Glaxx started draining energy from the star, most of the planet's crops were grown here. Now it's a frozen wasteland.

Many of Glaxx's soldiers are here playing winter sports. You must find some clothes to keep warm and disguise yourselves. Find 4 pairs of snow boots, 4 pairs of goggles, 4 snow hats and 4 gooth skin coats. Don't take anything that the soldiers are wearing.

Plib's ship is damaged beyond repair and his home is on the other side of the mountains. Plib says there is a tunnel that will take you there. Find the entrance to the tunnel.

The snow is too deep to walk through, but you must reach the tunnel. There is an abandoned snow craft half buried in the snow. Find the snow craft and its handlebars, and also find a shovel to dig them out. Put them together and head for the tunnel.

Find a pot of melted gooth's cheese and 6 crusts of bread to take with you.

5 hackey masks

7 ski sticks

7 hackey pucks

12

7 snow boards

9 two-headed ponguins

7 hackey sticks

6 gooths

14 slalom flags

Lava Luvvies

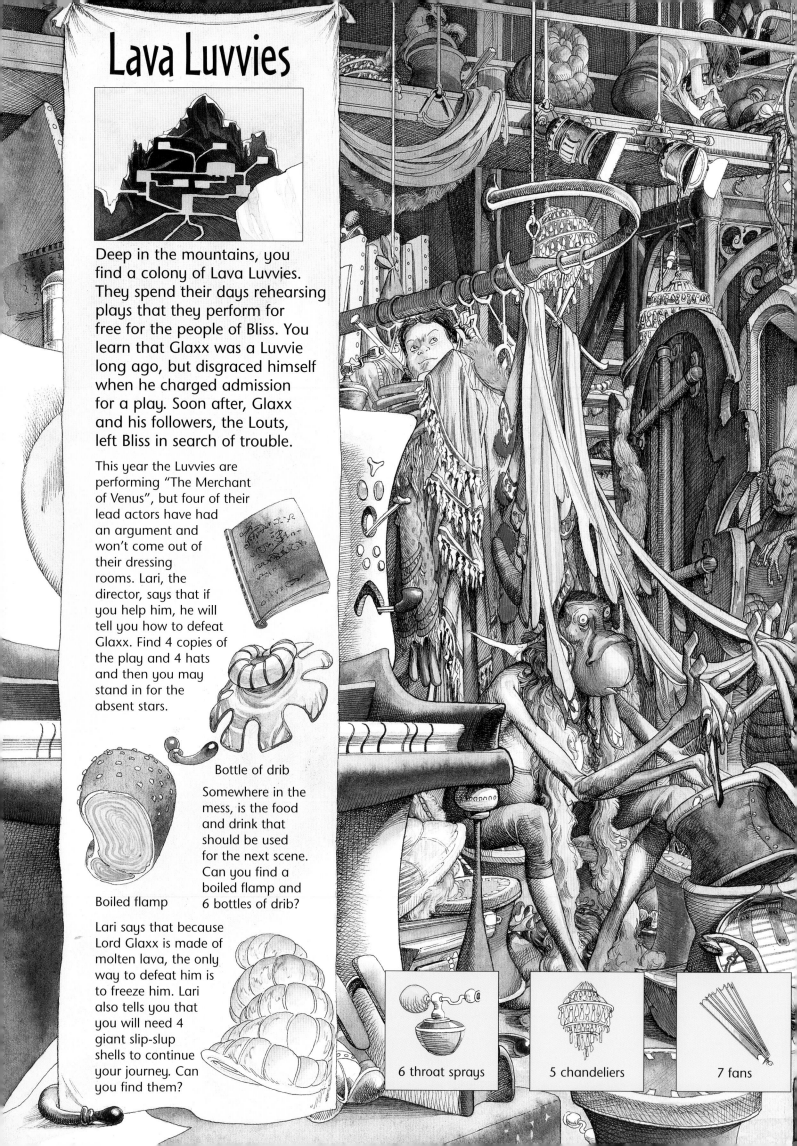

Deep in the mountains, you find a colony of Lava Luvvies. They spend their days rehearsing plays that they perform for free for the people of Bliss. You learn that Glaxx was a Luvvie long ago, but disgraced himself when he charged admission for a play. Soon after, Glaxx and his followers, the Louts, left Bliss in search of trouble.

This year the Luvvies are performing "The Merchant of Venus", but four of their lead actors have had an argument and won't come out of their dressing rooms. Lari, the director, says that if you help him, he will tell you how to defeat Glaxx. Find 4 copies of the play and 4 hats and then you may stand in for the absent stars.

Bottle of drib

Somewhere in the mess, is the food and drink that should be used for the next scene. Can you find a boiled flamp and 6 bottles of drib?

Boiled flamp

Lari says that because Lord Glaxx is made of molten lava, the only way to defeat him is to freeze him. Lari also tells you that you will need 4 giant slip-slup shells to continue your journey. Can you find them?

6 throat sprays

5 chandeliers

7 fans

13 sandbags

8 feather boas

10 hat boxes

2 pairs of binoculars

6 wigs

Loch Lung

Loch Lung is an ancient lake that is warmed by the rivers of lava that flow under it. The lake is very deep in places, and there are many strange creatures living in its depths. You are at the bottom of the lake, breathing the air trapped inside the slip-slup shells.

Many creatures that live in the lake eat giant slip-slups, which means you are in trouble if they catch you! Find 5 noctoquids and use them to keep the predators away. The noctoquids squirt clouds of foul-tasting ink when they are threatened.

With the shells on your heads, you can't see where you're going. It would be far too dangerous to continue on foot. There's an abandoned boat on the surface of the water. If you can find its anchor, you can swim to the surface using the rope as a guide. Then you can continue your journey in the boat.

Many fishermen have dropped food into the lake when their boats were capsized by a mysterious creature. There are 3 flasks and 3 lunch boxes somewhere in the lake. If the water hasn't seeped in, the food should still be good to eat.

8 loaches

2 live slip-slups

5 hairy narks

16

5 stone fish

8 squirms

6 hooks

5 eatles

10 blobbers

Ooh Aah Forest

Everything in the Ooh Aah Forest either stings or bites. The trees and plants are so dense in this part of the forest that the cold weather on the rest of the planet still hasn't reached it.

Just one bite from an Ooh Aah moskeet will put you to sleep for a week and a day. The only way to keep the moskeets away is by grating the seeds of a special plant that grows in the forest. Find 6 seeds and the seed grater.

Grater   Seed

It is very hard to find any food that is safe to eat. The easiest thing to do is to take food from the gimmy minkeys. There are 5 gimmy minkeys eating. Find them and snatch their food.

hider spiders are very bad tempered. If you step on one, it will drag you down a hole and eat you. There are 9 hider spiders to avoid.

You can get out of the forest by walking along the rope bridges, but if you meet a sneep, you must slide all the way along its back. Do not step over a sneep or it will bite you. Start with Harry and find a safe path out of the forest.

Sneep

6 munchers

7 sillypedes

8 pongflowers

11 nastyfungs

7 buzflits

7 bumpfruits

9 treefrubs

Blange

You have arrived at Plib's home town which is called Blange. Everyone is trying to keep warm in the frozen food factory. Before Glaxx started draining the star's energy, the Blissters used to freeze their crops in this factory and export the food to planets all over the galaxy.

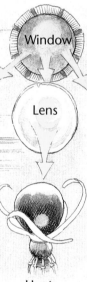

Window

Lens

Heater

The heating in the town has broken down because everything is solar powered, and the star doesn't have enough energy to make the machines work. If you can find a large magnifying lens, you may be able to concentrate enough power from the star to direct onto the solar panel that powers the factory heater.

To quick-freeze food, the Blissters used freezer cannons powered by energy crystals. The cannons would be ideal to use against the Lava Louts, along with the 6 crystals you collected earlier. There are 4 cannons and another crystal to find in the factory.

Peep

Most of the food has been eaten, but there are some frozen peeps left over. Find 6 peeps and allow them to defrost slowly near the factory heater.

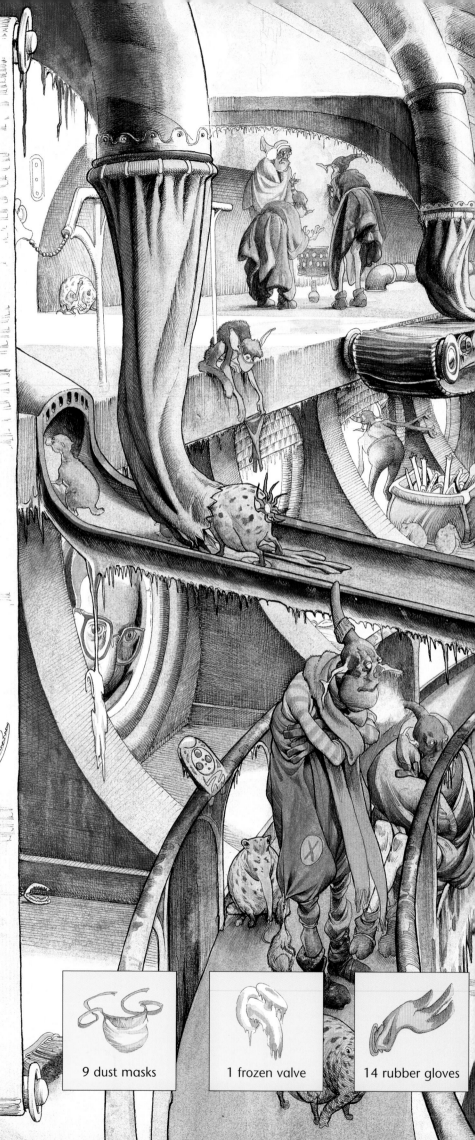

9 dust masks

1 frozen valve

14 rubber gloves

20

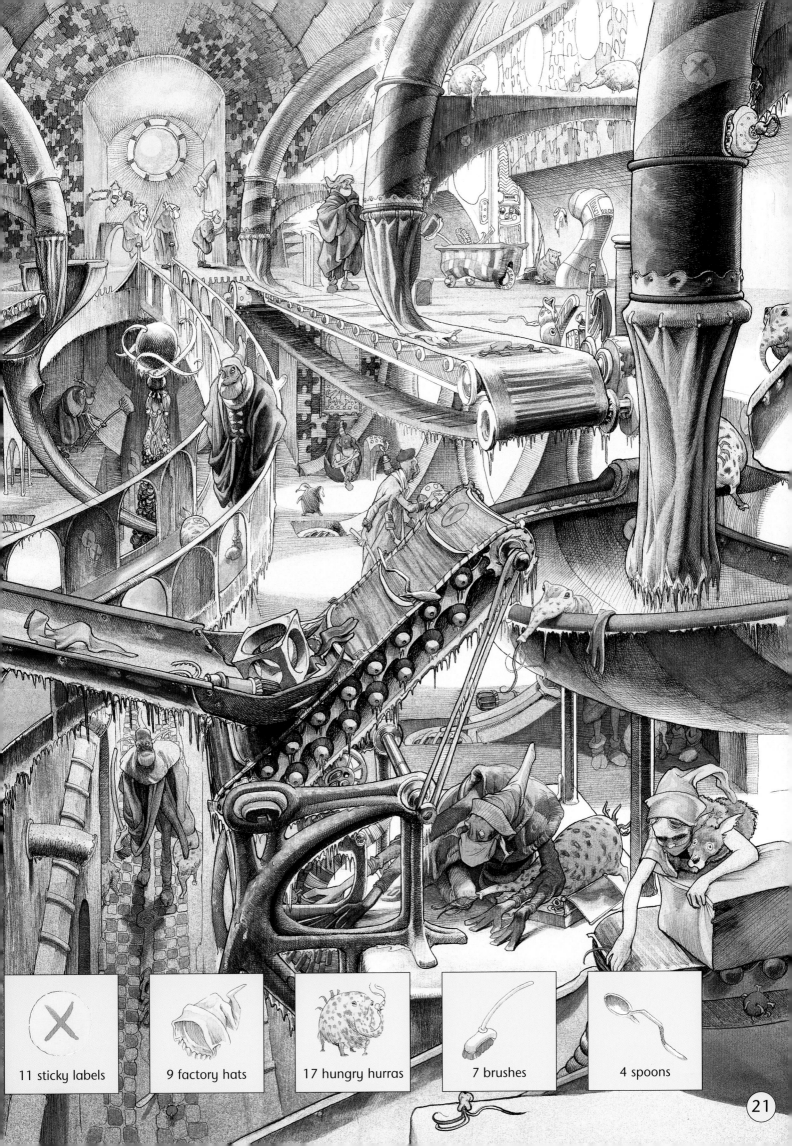

11 sticky labels

9 factory hats

17 hungry hurras

7 brushes

4 spoons

Blange Museum

The fastest and safest way to reach Glaxx's spaceship is by teleporting there. Unfortunately the town's teleporter isn't working due to the lack of energy. You have come to Blange Museum because there is a very old clockwork teleporter called the Jigger Jugger here. You may be able to make it work.

The museum is swarming with nasty flying creatures called crackacks. They must have broken a window to get in. Crackacks love to chew on old bones. Find 12 old bones and throw them out of the broken window. The crackacks will fly out after them.

The largest, smallest and strangest vegetables ever grown on Bliss are on display in the museum. Most of them have dried out and wouldn't be nice to eat, but there is one bluebibble that was put into the exhibition last week that might still be edible.

The Jigger Jugger is in the middle of the room. The key has been put away for safety. Find the key and use it to wind the machine. Then sit on the seats and think very hard about Glaxx's ship. (Don't forget to find the last 3 crystals before you go).

11 crackacks

8 saddles

5 energy bulbs

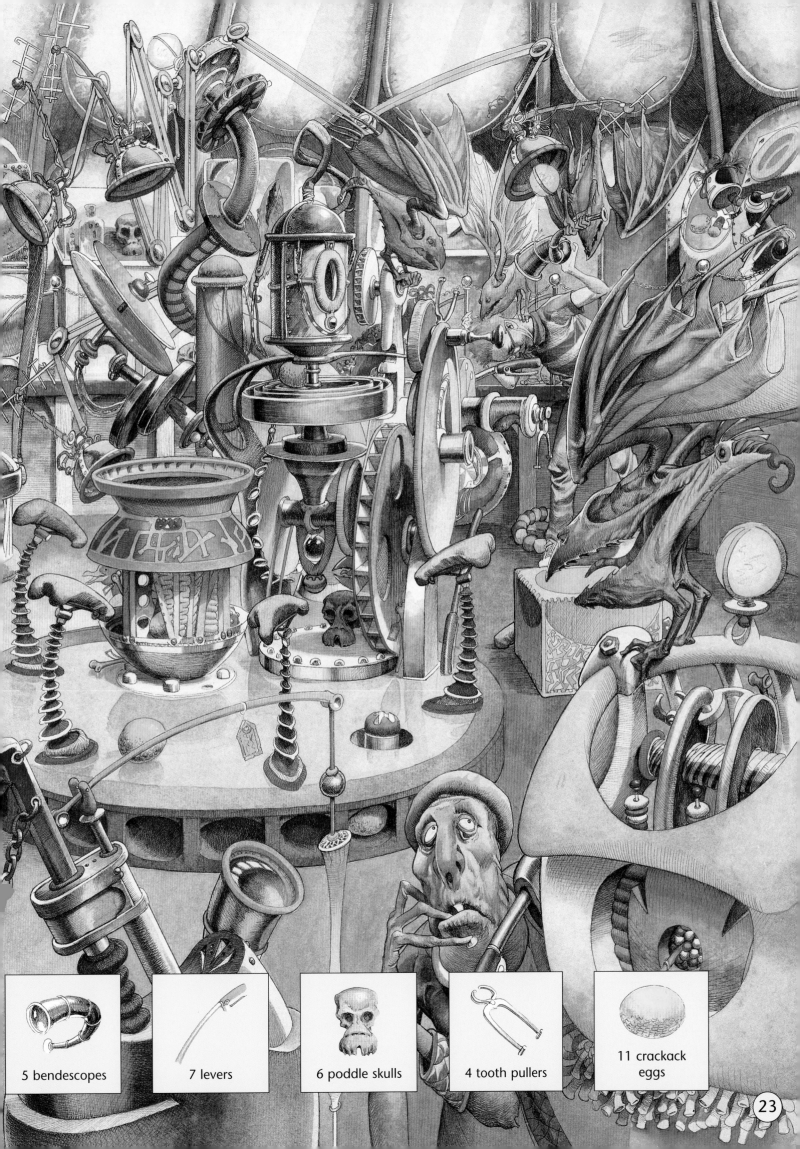

5 bendescopes

7 levers

6 poddle skulls

4 tooth pullers

11 crackack eggs

Glaxx's Ship

You've arrived in the transporter room of Glaxx's ship, but the Jigger Jugger's ancient machinery has caused the ship's own transporter to malfunction. Now it is transporting parts of Plib's and Harry's bodies around the room. You'll have to find their body parts and put them back together. Then you can freeze the Lava Louts with the freezer cannons.

Now you must shut the transporter down to stop any more Louts from coming up from the surface of the planet. There are 3 handles that control the transporter. You need to find them and pull them down.

Glaxx is in the Laser Room, draining more power from the star. To find the laser room, pick up a copy of the ship's guide. It contains useful information and a plan of the ship.

Can opener

There are many cans scattered around the room, but the food in most of them tastes horrible. The pokey blubber is not too bad, though. Find 1 can of pokey blubber and a can opener.

6 walky squawkys

5 window sprays

3 cans of lava

6 old meteors

8 space flies

7 cans of squeak

5 packets of bubble gum

8 ow guns

Laser Room

You have found your way to the Laser Room where the evil Lord Glaxx is draining the energy from the star with his powerful laser. You find that your freezer cannons don't have enough energy to freeze him, so you must find another way of stopping him from destroying the star completely.

First you must get Glaxx away from the laser. One of the Lava Louts' greatest fears are rock beetles which bite and crunch and chew their hard, stony skin. There are 7 beetle traps in the room. Each one contains an angry rock beetle. Find and open the traps and throw the beetles at Glaxx.

While Glaxx tries to get the beetles out of his clothes, find 4 space suits and put them on. Find and open the airlock, then hold on tight! Glaxx will be sucked out of the airlock into space where it is so cold, he will freeze and shatter into a million pieces.

Find the laser's gear shift lever. Put it into reverse and fire the laser. All the energy will transfer from the storage tanks into the star and Bliss will warm up again.

Now you can return to Bliss for a big party in the glorious sunshine before going home.

5 oil cans

10 T-pipes

21 grease monkeys

7 pressure valves | 5 oily rags | 6 grease cans | 7 oily combs | 5 valve handles

Star World 6–7

Plib 1

Jess 2

Harry 3

Plib's spaceship 4

Starburgers 5 6 7 8 9

Solarshakes 10 11 12
13 14

Space helmets 15 16 17
18 19 20 21

Roadrunners 22 23 24 25
26 27 28 29 30

Lollipops 31 32 33 34 35
36 37 38 39 40 41 42

Star World hats 43 44 45
46 47 48 49 50 51 52
53 54 55 56

Security guards 57 58 59
60 61 62 63 64 65 66

Prairie dogs 67 68 69 70
71 72 73 74 75

Balloons 76 77 78 79 80
81 82 83 84 85 86 87
88 89 90 91 92 93 94
95 96 97 98 99 100
101 102 103 104 105
106 107 108 109 110

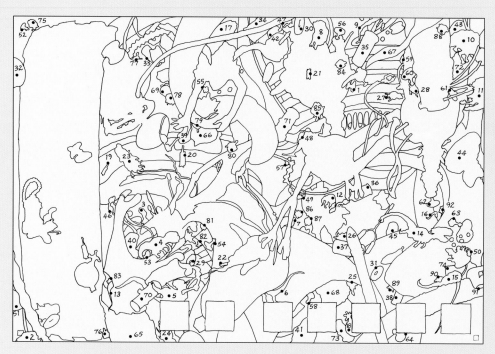

Plib's Ship 8–9

Gravity handle 1

Glibbers 2 3 4 5 6 7 8 9
10 11 12 13 14 15 16

Vacuum cleaner 17

Zoom drive 18

Zoom rods 19 20 21 22

Glimyubbers 23 24 25 26
27 28

Greeblows 29 30 31

Cans of de-icer 32 33 34
35 36 37 38

Moon boots 39 40 41 42
43 44 45

Pairs of goggles 46 47 48
49 50

Spare fuses 51 52 53 54
55 56 57 58 59 60 61
62 63 64

Travel blankets 65 66
67 68

Music cylinders 69 70 71
72 73 74

Air fresheners 75 76 77
78 79 80 81 82 83 84
85 86 87 88 89 90 91

Energy crystal 92

Space Station 10–11

Blue salads 1 2 3 4 5 6 7

Pizza slices 8 9 10 11 12
13 14 15 16 17 18 19

Fuel hose 20

Correct lever 21

Tool 22

Fuel cans 23 24 25 26 27
28 29 30

Crates 31 32 33 34 35 36
37 38 39 40

Waiters 41 42 43 44 45
46 47 48 49 50 51 52
53 54 55 56

Fuel tokens 57 58 59 60
61 62 63 64 65 66 67
68 69

Keys 70 71 72 73

Space horns 74 75 76 77
78 79

Pairs of furry dice 80 81
82 83 84 85 86 87 88

Glibber traps 89 90 91 92
93 94 95

Energy crystal 96

Button Jess should press
97

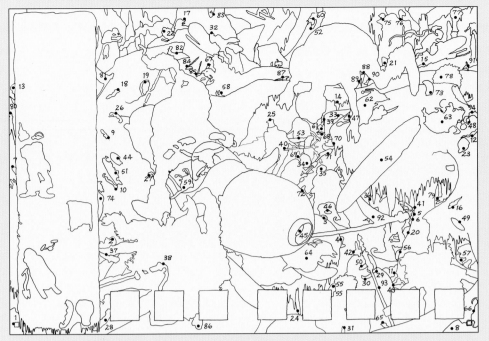

Ice Lands 12–13

Snow boots 1 2 3 4 5 6 7 8

Goggles 9 10 11 12

Snow hats 13 14 15 16

Gooth skin coats 17 18 19 20

Tunnel entrance 21

Snow craft 22

Handlebars 23

Shovel 24

Gooth's cheese 25

Crusts of bread 26 27 28 29 30 31

Hackey masks 32 33 34 35 36

Ski sticks 37 38 39 40 41 42 43

Hackey pucks 44 45 46 47 48 49 50

Snow boards 51 52 53 54 55 56 57

Ponguins 58 59 60 61 62 63 64 65 66

Hackey sticks 67 68 69 70 71 72 73

Gooths 74 75 76 77 78 79

Slalom flags 80 81 82 83 84 85 86 87 88 89 90 91 92 93

Energy crystal 94

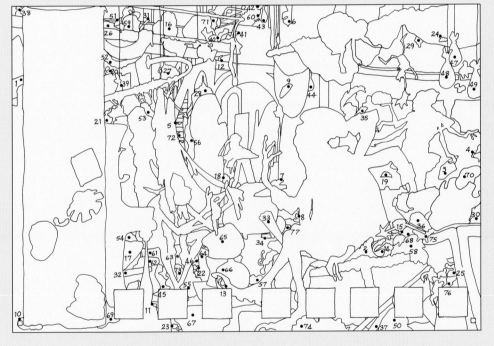

Lava Luvvies 14–15

Copies of the play 1 2 3 4

Hats 5 6 7 8

Boiled flamp 9

Bottles of drib 10 11 12 13 14 15

Giant slip-slup shells 16 17 18 19

Throat sprays 20 21 22 23 24 25

Chandeliers 26 27 28 29 30

Fans 31 32 33 34 35 36 37

Sandbags 38 39 40 41 42 43 44 45 46 47 48 49 50

Feather boas 51 52 53 54 55 56 57 58

Hat boxes 59 60 61 62 63 64 65 66 67 68

Binoculars 69 70

Wigs 71 72 73 74 75 76

Energy crystal 77

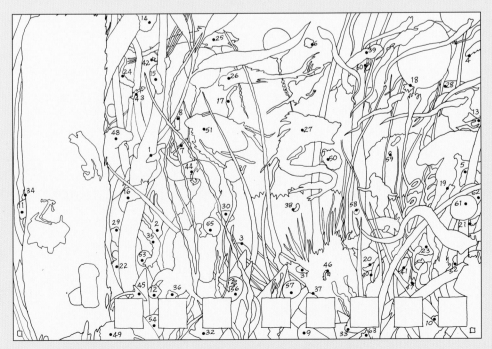

Loch Lung 16–17

Noctoquids 1 2 3 4 5

Boat 6

Anchor 7

Flasks 8 9 10

Lunch boxes 11 12 13

Loaches 14 15 16 17 18 19 20 21

Live slip-slups 22 23

Hairy narks 24 25 26 27 28

Stone fish 29 30 31 32 33

Squirms 34 35 36 37 38 39 40 41

Hooks 42 43 44 45 46 47

Eatles 48 49 50 51 52

Blobbers 53 54 55 56 57 58 59 60 61 62

Energy crystal 63

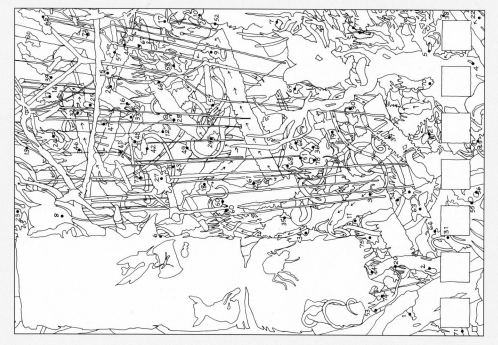

Ooh Aah Forest 18–19

Seeds 1 2 3 4 5 6

Grater 7

Gimmy monkeys (eating) 8 9 10 11 12

Hider spiders 13 14 15 16 17 18 19 20 21

Harry's route starts at 22. The arrows show his safe route out of the forest.

Treefrubs 23 24 25 26 27 28 29 30 31

Bumpfruits 32 33 34 35 36 37 38

Buzflits 39 40 41 42 43 44 45

Nastyfungs 46 47 48 49 50 51 52 53 54 55 56

Pong flowers 57 58 59 60 61 62 63 64

Sillypedes 65 66 67 68 69 70 71

Munchers 72 73 74 75 76 77

Energy crystal 78

Blange 20–21

Magnifying lens 1

Freezer cannons 2 3 4 5

Energy crystal 6

Peeps 7 8 9 10 11 12

Dust masks 13 14 15 16 17 18 19 20 21

Frozen valve 22

Rubber gloves 23 24 25 26 27 28 29 30 31 32 33 34 35 36

Sticky labels 37 38 39 40 41 42 43 44 45 46 47

Factory hats 48 49 50 51 52 53 54 55 56

Hungry hurras 57 58 59 60 61 62 63 64 65 66 67 68 69 70 71 72 73

Brushes 74 75 76 77 78 79 80

Spoons 81 82 83 84

Blange Museum 22–23

Old bones 1 2 3 4 5 6 7 8 9 10 11 12

Bluebibble 13

Jigger Jugger key 14

Crackacks 15 16 17 18 19 20 21 22 23 24 25

Saddles 26 27 28 29 30 31 32 33

Energy bulbs 34 35 36 37 38

Bendescopes 39 40 41 42 43

Levers 44 45 46 47 48 49 50

Poddle skulls 51 52 53 54 55 56

Tooth pullers 57 58 59 60

Crackack eggs 61 62 63 64 65 66 67 68 69 70 71

Energy crystals 72 73 74